Written and Illustrated by Ali Currie

For Finlay and Faith. Be Bold.

With thanks to Stuart for sharing his mad dreams and boundless enthusiasm
and to the army of family and friends who have helped Mimi find her voice.

First Edition published in 2017
by Hoolet Publishing in Glasgow, Scotland
For more information, visit *www.hoolet.scot*

ISBN: 978-0-9957548-1-2

The world was choking on the furious fumes of
A MILLION MARVELLOUS MALFUNCTIONING MACHINES.

Smog and smoke were a daily distraction, making classrooms of children cough and splutter sporadically. Something had to be done, a solution had to be sought.

Prime Minister Merryweather, a funny and friendly looking fella, created a competition with a most prestigious prize.

"We are calling on the most magnificent minds to share their most incredible ideas," the Prime Minister proclaimed.

"An incredible idea?" mused Mini Mimi. It seemed to her that these magnificent minds had missed a very simple solution.

The pupils at Peppermint Primary School in
Little Littleton had tuned in to watch the Prime Minister
announce this astounding country-wide competition.

Mini Mimi, who was normally quite quiet,
raised her hand and cleared her throat.

"Miss Twiddlewiddle," announced Mimi,
"There seems to be a VERY SIMPLE SOLUTION."

"BUT NOTHING, MIMI"

"Don't you worry your pretty little head Mimi," replied Miss Twiddlewiddle. "This is a big problem for big people with big brains, not for little ladies from Little Littleton."

Mimi was miffed: "BUT MISS..."

"BUT NOTHING, MIMI," interrupted Miss Twiddlewiddle. "The best I'd suggest is that you be patient and perhaps one day, maybe, you could possibly participate in prestigious scientific competitions."

As disappointed as Mimi was, she was DETERMINED to be heard.

She prepared a plan and persuaded her primary school principal to take her class to the competition final.

Three thousand, three hundred and thirty-three of the best, most brilliant brains had supplied suggestions. Prime Minister Merryweather personally picked three participants to present their projects.

In an awesome auditorium, Mimi, her classmates and a large audience arrived to be amazed by the

ALL-STAR SCIENTIFIC SUPERHEROES.

First up was Dr Doodwhackle from Dundee, wearing a wonderful white waistcoat.

He spoke with a particularly posh accent and wore silly-looking circular spectacles.

Undoubtedly dedicated, he gave the impression that his immense intellect would be generously given to the greater good.

MASTER MAKER
OFFICIAL ENTRY FORM

Name:

Dr Dundas Doodwhackle PhD.
from Downtown Dundee

Employer:

Doodwhackle Widgets & Wizziwigs Ltd.

Likes:

Doodling doohickeys, dancing in
Dundee discotheques and doing
dangerous domino demonstrations.

Dr Doodwhackle's machine was called the
WONDERFUL WHIROMATIC 1000.

It would whir and purr with smooth, soothing sounds, slowly sucking up all the smog without a hint of hindrance.

"My remarkable, revolutionary machine is absolutely necessary and will be worth every single penny," presented Doodwhackle.

"Furthermore," he followed, "it is unquestionably an absolute bargain at just a QUIZILLION QUID."

"A quizillion quid?" the competition committee considered. "We could never afford the funds for this Wonderful Whiromatic 1000," and without one second of worry, the whole committee cried...

And next up was Professor Penelope Pinopin from Pontypridd who wore a peacock-like poncho, populated with plenty patterns in courageous colours.

Penelope was brighter than the most brilliant bulb. Her manner was mild, sweet and sensitive. There was a certain certainty to every sentence she stated; she was precise, if peculiar.

MASTER MAKER
OFFICIAL ENTRY FORM

Name:

Prof Penelope Pinopin
from Pontypridd Promenade

Employer:

Pen Pin Products and Purchasers plc.

Likes:

Painting poppies in Paris, pouring pea flavoured tea into porcelain pots and passing time in Portugese potteries.

Professor Pinopin's machine was proclaimed the

PRICELESS POOP PROCESSOR (PATENT PENDING).

"Behold," boomed the brainiac, "my bold, ground-breaking behemoth. Its pistons pump while it squeezes down the dung. Poop is pushed through many multiple pipes and the pressure powers a family of fans that wafts the smog high into the sky."

However, the machine's stinky smells seemed to seep and creep and cling to the crowd's clothes. The gathered masses were quite aghast. Half of the theatre fell foul of the funky fumes.

The competition committee's senior spokeswoman, Mrs Sally Sanasar, recovered her composure and coughed a conclusive...

...NEXT!

MRS SALLY SANASAR

Sir Simon Sizzleson stepped onto the stage next. This eccentric entrepreneur wore a suit that suited him as much as a snake suits sunglasses. That is to say, not one little bit.

His hair was a slick side parting of beaming blonde hair. A massive moustache looped around his mouth and fabulously framed a grimy grin. His prickly personality and mean manner were particularly unpleasant.

MASTER MAKER
OFFICIAL ENTRY FORM

Name:

Sir Simon Sizzleson
from Southampton Seafront

Employer:

Sizzleson of Southampton and Sons.

Likes:

Sauntering slowly, sailing silently in smooth seas and settling on the sofa for Saturday siestas.

Sizzleson's machine, the SOUNDSATIONAL SMOG SMASHER, started with a crash and a bash. The roar and ruckus of the deafening device shook the room and everyone in it.

"THE SOUNDWAVES, YOU SEE," shouted Sir Sizzleson, "SHAKE AND BREAK THE SMOKE INTO TEENY TINY PILLOW-LIKE PUFFS. AS SOON AS THEY ARE SUPER SMALL THE MACHINE SIMPLY SUCKS UP AND STORES THE SMOG."

"WHAT DID HE SAY?" queried one of the committee.

"I'M SORRY I CAN'T HEAR A THING," announced another.

A decision was determined by the Deputy Chairman, Dr Douglas Chizzlewick. "WHILE YOU SHOULD BE VERY, VERY PROUD, YOUR MACHINE IS MUCH, MUCH TOO LOUD!" and together the committee cried a collective...

...NEXT!

DR DOUGLAS CHIZZLEWICK

But there was no one next. Not one of the super science mega minds had managed to mend the awfully atrocious air.

Just as the last of the creative creations was wheeled off stage, a tiny little voice could just about be heard. Everyone piped down and Mini Mimi spoke up.

"EXCUSE ME, I HAVE AN IDEA."

"You have an idea?" came a chorus from the curious crowd.

"Yes, I have an idea. Would you like to hear it?" asked Mimi.

An "erm-ahh-uhm…" came from the confused committee.

"I'll take that 'erm-ahh-uhm' as an 'uh-huh', shall I?" insisted the increasingly impressive Mini Mimi.

"May I propose a product that quietly turns out amazingly aromatic air," announced Mimi. "My clever contraption effortlessly absorbs the foul fumes and is really, REALLY (really) reliable. And what's more, this doohickey will absolutely, positively not cost you a crate-full of cash."

"So, what is this marvellous machine?" asked Admiral Archibald Agogo, Chair of the competition committee.

"Ah, you see sir, we do not need malfunctioning monstrosities to improve the air," announced the lively little lady.

"MAY I PROUDLY PRESENT THE PERFECTLY PRACTICAL AND TERRIFICALLY TREMENDOUS…

ADMIRAL ARCHIBALD AGOGO

"SO, WHAT IS THIS MARVELLOUS MACHINE?"

"What we need are forests full of trees,"
Mimi announced. "A jolly jungle or ninety-nine
are absolutely necessary."

"A tree, you see, absorbs ill air and turns out tons of
top-notch fabulous fresh air," Mimi declared. "For the
fashion conscious, these trees come in all shapes and
sizes to suit your surroundings and they can be planted
pretty much any which where."

"If we stop cutting down and clearing our forests we
can clean up the air. We also need to stop continually
concocting crazy contraptions that create these
air polluting plumes," pleaded the petite pupil.

MASTER
MAKER

"AMAZING!" "FANTASTIC!" "OUTSTANDING!"

the competition committee cried and
a standing ovation was immediately supplied.

Mini Mimi was made Master Maker, but not for making a machine.
No, she won her award for making everyone see that many marvellous
minds can sometimes miss the perfect proposal that already exists.

Anyone can have an incredible idea and while it may seem silly at first,
it could be the most impressive, most important idea ever.

And what's MORE,
the BIGGEST ideas can often
come from the LITTLEST people.

If you enjoyed this book, you may also be interested in the world of The Kelvinhill Kids. This gang is keen on adventures and don't let anything stop them from enjoying days out.

For more information about The Kelvinhill Kids, Mini Mimi, printable colouring pages, videos and audio, please visit www.hoolet.scot